Snail Trail

Level 3A

Written by Sally Grindley
Illustrated by Mike Phillips
Reading Consultant: Betty Franchi

About Phonics

Spoken English uses more than 40 speech sounds.
Each sound is called a *phoneme*. Some phonemes relate
to a single letter (d-o-g) and others to combinations
of letters (sh-ar-p). When a phoneme is written down,
it is called a *grapheme*. Teaching these sounds, matching
them to their written form, and sounding out words for
reading is the basis of phonics.

Early phonics instruction gives children the tools to sound
out, blend, and say the words without having to rely on
memory or guesswork. This instruction gives children the
confidence and ability to read unfamiliar words, helping
them progress toward independent reading.

About the Consultant

Betty Franchi is an American educator with a Bachelor's Degree in Elementary and Middle Education as well as a Master's Degree in Special Education. Betty holds a National Boards for Professional Teaching Standards certification. Throughout her 24 years as a teacher, she has studied and developed an expertise in Phonetic Awareness and has implemented phonetic strategies, teaching many young children to read, including students with special needs.

Reading tips

This book focuses on the *ai* sound.

Tricky and/or new words in this book

Any words in bold may have unusual spellings or are new and have not yet been introduced.

> **Tricky and/or new words in this book**
>
> ## the for she
> ## of to

Extra ways to have fun with this book

After the readers have finished the story, ask them questions about what they have just read.

What does Gail do with the snail in her pail?
Why does Gail have a shock at the end of the story?

Make flashcards for each of the sounds within the pronunciation guide. This will help reinforce letter/ sound matches.

I'm a fast reader. I like to read on the go!

A Pronunciation Guide

This grid highlights the sounds used in the story and offers a guide on how to say them.

s	a	t	p	i
as in sat	as in ant	as in tin	as in pig	as in ink
n	c	e	h	r
as in net	as in cat	as in egg	as in hen	as in rat
m	d	g	o	u
as in mug	as in dog	as in get	as in ox	as in up
l	f	b	j	v
as in log	as in fan	as in bag	as in jug	as in van
w	z	y	k	qu
as in wet	as in zip	as in yet	as in kit	as in quick
x	ff	ll	ss	zz
as in box	as in off	as in ball	as in kiss	as in buzz
ck	pp	nn	rr	gg
as in duck	as in puppy	as in bunny	as in arrow	as in egg
dd	bb	tt	sh	ch
as in daddy	as in chubby	as in attic	as in shop	as in chip
th	th	ng	nk	le
as in them	as in the	as in sing	as in sunk	as in bottle
ai				
as in rain				

Be careful not to add an /uh/ sound to /s/, /t/, /p/, /c/, /h/, /r/, /m/, /d/, /g/, /l/, /f/ and /b/. For example, say /ff/ not /fuh/ and /sss/ not /suh/.

A snail slid from a drain
in **the** rain.

The snail slid in the paint and made a trail. The trail is on a pail.

The trail is on a train.

Gail, the maid, spots the trail.

"This is such a pain!" wails Gail.
"A snail has made a trail."

Gail gets a pail and scrubs the trail.
But the trail stays the same!

"The snail trail has left
a paint stain," wails Gail.

Gail waits **for** the snail.

She has laid a trail **of** bait.

The snail is back!

The snail sees the bait.

The snail slid **to** the trail
of bait. Munch, munch.

Gail pops the snail in the pail.

Gail sets the snail on the grass.

Gail cannot wait to get back.

But Gail has a big shock.

A second snail has made a trail!

OVER **48** TITLES IN SIX LEVELS
Betty Franchi recommends...

Some titles from Level 1

Bad Rat — 978 1 84898 747 0

The Best Gift — 978 1 84898 750 0

Clint and Grant Play I-Spy — 978 1 84898 752 4

Bret and Grandma's Trip! — 978 1 84898 751 7

Some titles from Level 2

Wish Fish — 978 1 84898 755 5

Chuck and Duck — 978 1 84898 756 2

Pink Bunny — 978 1 84898 760 9

Let's go to the Swings — 978 1 84898 759 3

Other titles to enjoy from Level 3

Bart's Go-Cart — 978 1 84898 768 5

Queen Ella's Feet — 978 1 84898 764 7

Puff Flies — 978 1 84898 765 4

An Hachette Company
First Published in the United States by TickTock, an imprint of Octopus Publishing Group.
www.octopusbooksusa.com

Copyright © Octopus Publishing Group Ltd 2013

Distributed in the US by
Hachette Book Group USA
237 Park Avenue, New York NY 10017, USA

Distributed in Canada by
Canadian Manda Group
165 Dufferin Street, Toronto, Ontario, Canada M6K 3H6

ISBN 978 1 84898 763 0

Printed and bound in China
10 9 8 7 6 5 4 3 2 1